W9-BDT-168

The Mother's Day Mice

The Mother's Day Mice

BY EVE BUNTING & ILLUSTRATED BY JAN BRETT

CLARION BOOKS
New York

To Dana and her mother
with love
—E.B.

To Joseph
—J.B.

Clarion Books
a Houghton Mifflin Company imprint
215 Park Avenue South, New York, NY 10003
Text Copyright © 1986 by Eve Bunting
Illustrations Copyright © 1986 by Jan Brett
All rights reserved.

For information about permission to reproduce selections from
this book, write to Permissions, Houghton Mifflin Company,
215 Park Avenue South, New York, NY 10003.

Printed in Singapore

Library of Congress Cataloging-in-Publication Data
Bunting, Eve, 1928-
The Mother's Day Mice.
Summary: Three little mouse brothers go into the meadow to find
a present for their mother but it is the littlest mouse that comes up
with the most unusual gift of all.
[1. Gifts—Fiction. 2. Mice—Fiction.]
I. Brett, Jan. 1949-   ill.   II. Title.
PZ7.B91527Mp   1986   [E]   85-13991
ISBN 0-89919-387-0   PA ISBN 0-89919-702-7

TWP 40 39 38 37 36 35 34 33 32

Biggest Little Mouse wakened first. It was early morning and still almost dark. He tugged gently on the whiskers of Middle Mouse, who slept next to him. "It's Mother's Day," he whispered. "Time to get up and go for our presents."

Middle Mouse tugged gently on the whiskers of Little Mouse, who slept between him and the wall. "Mother's Day," he whispered.

They crept out of bed and tiptoed past Mother's room.

Outside, one star still slept in the sky. They stopped to wash paws and faces in the pail of water Mother kept by the front door.

Biggest studied his watch. "We have two hours before Mother wakes up. Middle and I know what *we're* getting for her and where to find it." He looked at Little Mouse and waited.

"I know what I'm getting, too," Little Mouse said. "Honeysuckle!"

Biggest shook his head. "Little Mouse! Honeysuckle grows only on Honeysuckle Cottage. And we know who lives in Honeysuckle Cottage. You'll have to find something else for Mother."

Little Mouse wanted to argue, but Biggest was already lining them up, one behind the other. "Hold tails and be quiet as we go," he said. "The dark has dangers for little mice."

They ran across the meadow. Little Mouse liked the tough, smooth feel of his brother's tail. He thought the three of them, joined together, must be long as a snake. He didn't want to think about snakes, though.

The edges of sky were streaked with morning. A red fox passed them on his way home. They crouched till the white tip of his tail disappeared in the trees.

"Grrr!" Little Mouse said fiercely. "Who's afraid of *him*?" But his voice was so weak that he couldn't hear it himself.

An owl sheared above them as they lay hidden in the long grass. Little Mouse kept his eyes tight closed. If he couldn't see the owl, the owl couldn't see him.

"You didn't have to squeeze my tail so *hard*," Middle Mouse told him when they stood up.

"I thought you might be frightened," Little Mouse said. "I was telling you I was here."

Middle Mouse sniffed.

A strawberry patch grew at the edge of the meadow.

"There's *my* surprise for Mother," Middle Mouse said. "She loves strawberries. She says the first ones taste of summer coming."

Biggest Mouse boosted him so he could get the roundest, reddest berry from the top. Its weight tipped him backward as he carried it.

"*My* surprise is here, too," Biggest Mouse said. He picked a dandelion fluff ball and held it high by its milky stem. "It's a wish flower. A wish flower for Mother."

Little Mouse thought the fluff ball was as beautiful as a spinning of spiders' webs. He could see the sky through it.

"Mother will love it," Little Mouse said. "Now can we go for the honeysuckle? We have time. And maybe *he* won't be there."

Biggest Mouse sighed. "We'll go look. But only because you're the littlest and it's Mother's Day. And we won't go close. Cat is *always* there."

Cat *was* there.

He lay on the porch of Honeysuckle Cottage, monstrously big, monstrously black. When he yawned his mouth was a dark, spiked cave. Little Mouse could see it clearly even though they weren't too close.

"Maybe he'll leave soon," Little Mouse whispered. He pulled his eyes away from Cat to the honeysuckle that twined around the porch. Honeysuckle for Mother.

Inside the cottage someone was playing a piano. The tune was "Twinkle, Twinkle, Little Star." *Dum dee, dum dee, dum dee da. Dum dee, dum dee, dum dee da.*

"Maybe Cat likes to lie in the sun and listen to music," Little Mouse whispered. "Maybe the person will stop playing soon, and Cat will go away." He sniffed the honeysuckle air and pretended not to see Biggest Mouse check the time.

Dum dee, dum dee, dum dee da.

"That person is *not* going to stop playing," Middle muttered. He set his strawberry on the ground and a beetle came on the run.

Middle picked it up again and shooed the beetle away.

Little Mouse began creeping toward the cottage on his belly.

Biggest yanked him back by his tail. "Stop that! Anyway, it's time to go. What if Mother wakes up on Mother's Day and all her little mice are missing?"

"Or eaten?" Middle added.

"We have to go," Biggest said. "I'm sorry, Little Mouse."

But inside Little Mouse's head something had started to beat. Something wonderful that was the beginning of an idea. Something better than honeysuckle.

"It's all right," Little Mouse said.

The sun made a pink path across the meadow as they ran for home.

"Bring her a daisy," Biggest said over his shoulder. "She likes daisies."

"Bring her a rock," Middle puffed. "A small rock that's not hard to carry."

"They're nice," Little Mouse said. "But they're not special enough for this special day." He *had* something special, though. He had it strong and firm in his mind when they got home.

Biggest stood the fluff ball in a jar beside Mother's chair.

Middle put the strawberry on a blue dish on the table. "I'm glad I didn't roll it," he said. "Sometimes I wanted to. But I carried it all the way and it isn't even squished." He glanced sideways at Little Mouse. "The strawberry can be from you, too, Little Mouse."

"And the fluff ball will be from both of us," Biggest said.

Little Mouse smiled. "Thank you. But I brought something of my own." He thought it was funny when his brothers looked all around and then rolled their eyes at each other. "Something I kept hidden," he said.

Biggest Mouse held up a warning paw. "Shh! Mother's coming."

"Happy Mother's Day," they all shouted when she came in the kitchen, and Mother said: "Why! You remembered!"

"Remembered? We almost got eaten three...." Middle began, but Biggest poked him hard. Sometimes Middle talked too much.

Mother blew on the fluff ball and it exploded into a million beautiful, feathery seeds.

"Did you make a wish?" Biggest Mouse asked.

"Yes. A wonderful wish."

Mother cut the strawberry in four pieces. "I love strawberries," she said. "The first ones taste of summer coming."

She nibbled on an edge of berry and closed her eyes and Little Mouse knew she was tasting sunshine and sweet corn and the cold waters of Meadow Stream.

"Now ME!" he said. He was so excited he thought he might explode, like the fluff ball, into a million pieces.

The music he'd heard at Honeysuckle Cottage was loud in his mind and he clasped his paws and began to sing. He sang the words he'd thought of as they ran home.

We have brought a song to say,
Happy, happy Mother's Day.
No one's mother is so nice,
Love from all your little mice.

"That was wonderful," Mother said when he finished.

How astonished his brothers were! They'd thought he had nothing, and all the time he'd had *this*.

"Was it better than honeysuckle?" Little Mouse asked.

"Much better," Mother said. "Honeysuckle doesn't last forever. A song does."

"Was it the best of all your surprises?" As soon as he asked that, Little Mouse felt mean. "The song is from all of us," he added quickly.

Mother smiled. "All my surprises were lovely. You each brought me something different and you each brought me something the same. Do you know what that was, Little Mouse?"

Little Mouse knew. They'd brought her their love.

Mother opened her arms wide, and they ran to her.

"Let's sing Little Mouse's song," she said.

Mother and her three little mice swayed together as they sang. And the kitchen was warm with wishes, and summer coming, and music, and love.